Harry Potter™

HOGWARTS

A MOVIE SCRAPBOOK

WIZARDING WORLD

Random House ⌂ New York

An Insight Editions Book

CONTENTS

INTRODUCTION

Welcome to Hogwarts!

Every year on September 1, students returned to Hogwarts School of Witchcraft and Wizardry to learn new magical spells, study magical plants and creatures, and acquire additional knowledge to defend themselves against the Dark Arts. As the phenomenon of J.K. Rowling's Harry Potter book series grew, children of all ages waited for their Acceptance Letter to the wizarding school. The Harry Potter films gave everyone the chance to "attend" Hogwarts, which was brought to life by designers, decorators, craftspeople, and artists.

Production designer Stuart Craig had a sturdy York stone floor laid down in the Great Hall, which lasted through ten years of student duels, feasts, and dances. Set decorator Stephenie McMillan sought to add magic to even the most mundane items, such as blackboards whose "feet" were shod in boots. Graphic designers Miraphora Mina and Eduardo Lima studied with bookbinders to learn where books gain their worst wear and tear. Twenty to thirty copies of each required textbook were created, plus a few extras in case some got damaged. Costume designers Judianna Makovsky and Jany Temime designed robes for daily and formal wear and uniforms for a sport that took place in the air. Prop modeler Pierre Bohanna supervised the creation of wands, brooms, and potion bottles. And an incredibly talented cast of actors brought the students and a faculty of the best—and worst—teachers to life.

Every school year at Hogwarts brought new friends and adventures, tests and trials, and no small number of surprises. So gather your quills and parchment— it's time to go behind the scenes at Hogwarts!

FIRST YEAR STUDENTS WILL REQUIRE:

1. Three sets of plain work robes
2. One plain pointed hat for day wear
3. One pair of dragon-hide gloves

AND THE FOLLOWING SET BOOKS:

1. 'The Standard Book of Spells' by Miranda Goshawk
2. 'One Thousand Magical Herbs and Fungi' by Phyllida Spore
3. 'A History of Magic' by Bathilda Bagshot
4. 'Magical Theory' by Adalbert Waffling
5. 'A Beginner's Guide to Transfiguration' by Emeric Switch
6. 'Magical Drafts and Potions' by Arsenius Jigger
7. 'Fantastic Beasts and Where to Find Them' by Newt Scamander
8. 'The Dark Forces: A Guide to Self-Protection' by Quentin Trimble

ALL STUDENTS MUST BE EQUIPPED WITH:

1. One Wand
2. One standard 'Size 2' pewter cauldron
...and may bring, if they desire, either an owl, a cat, or a toad.

Lucinda Thomsonicle-Pocus,
Chief Attendant of Witchcraft Provisions

HOGWARTS SCHOOL of WITCHCRAFT & WIZARDRY
Headmaster: Albus Dumbledore, D.Wiz., X.J.(sorc.), S.of Mag.Q.

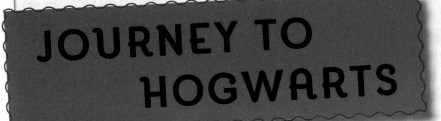

JOURNEY TO HOGWARTS

Hogwarts Acceptance Letter

First-year students of Hogwarts School of Witchcraft and Wizardry, an institution over one thousand years old hidden in the Scottish Highlands, are sent an Acceptance Letter via owl. Harry Potter's letter is delivered to the home of his Muggle relatives, the Dursleys. But the Dursleys don't want Harry to find out he's a wizard and try to keep the letter from him.

To: MR. H. POTTER,
  THE CUPBOARD UNDER THE STAIRS,
  4, PRIVET DRIVE,
  LITTLE WHINGING,
  SURREY

Dear Mr Potter......

We are pleased to inform you that you have been accepted at Hogwarts School of Witchcraft and Wizardry.

Students shall be required to report to the Chamber of Reception upon arrival, the dates for which shall be duly advised.

Dear Harry Potter,

Please be reminded that you must board the Hogwarts Express as usual from King's Cross Platform 9 3/4 for prompt departure on September the first at 09.34.

SECOND YEAR STUDENTS WILL REQUIRE:
1. *The Standard Book of Spells*, Grade 2 by Miranda Goshawk
2. *Break with a Banshee* by Gilderoy Lockhart
3. *Gadding with Ghouls* by Gilderoy Lockhart
4. *Holidays with Hags* by Gilderoy Lockhart
5. *Travels with Trolls* by Gilderoy Lockhart
6. *Voyages with Vampires* by Gilderoy Lockhart
7. *Wanderings with Werewolves* by Gilderoy Lockhart
8. *Year with the Yeti* by Gilderoy Lockhart

...in addition to your standard Wizarding equipment, as requ[...]
your first year.

[...]rm.

School Supplies

First-year students are required to bring a wand, robes, and equipment for classes in their trunk, and may bring an owl, a cat, or a toad. Set decorator Stephenie McMillan and her team located the students' trunks at antique stores and thrift shops. "The main characters' trunks had their initials and the school stamp," says Stephenie. "And then we had to find cages for owls and rats and cats." For days before filming of the first movie began, Stephenie's assistants went to pet shops trying to find different-shaped baskets and cages. The set decoration and prop departments also needed to produce items that wouldn't typically be available in large numbers in the Muggle world, such as brooms and cauldrons.

Getting to Hogwarts
Platform 9¾ at King's Cross Station

The Hogwarts Express transports new and returning students to Hogwarts every year, leaving from Platform 9¾ in King's Cross station, London. Director Chris Columbus wanted the audiences to feel like they also were going through the brick wall to the platform, so he filmed Daniel Radcliffe passing through a hollow one.

Today there is a luggage cart stuck in one of the walls at King's Cross station, placed there as a tribute to Harry Potter.

No. 257
Ticket to be shown upon demand
for ONE WAY travel
Platform 9¾
LONDON to HOGWARTS
Platform 9¾
Issued subject to the Rules & Regulations of the Hogwarts Express Railway Authorities

Hogwarts Express

Harry Potter meets his best friends, Ron Weasley and Hermione Granger, played by Rupert Grint and Emma Watson, on the Hogwarts Express. "In the train carriage where Harry and Ron first meet," says Rupert, "we were sitting opposite each other, and we were constantly giggling. We couldn't film it together, in fact, so we had to do it separately." Director Chris Columbus played Harry's part when they were filming Rupert, and then he played Ron to film Daniel Radcliffe.

EXTERIOR: TRAIN

"We didn't shoot the scene interiors on a real train traveling through Scotland," explains production designer Stuart Craig. So window views of the Scottish Highlands were filmed from real moving trains containing cameras, and aerial shots were taken from helicopters. These were then added to the scenes digitally. There were also actors wearing costumes on the real trains, so the compartments were occupied. Storyboards drawn for *Harry Potter and the Half-Blood Prince* give directions for filming the exterior of the train based on the needs of the scene.

Each school year introduces a different way for the students to get to—and into—Hogwarts castle. In *Harry Potter and the Sorcerer's Stone*, first-year students arrive via small, three–person boats that glide across the Black Lake. In *Harry Potter and the Deathly Hallows – Part 2*, viewers got to see inside the Boathouse. Stephenie McMillan's set decoration department provided seventy oars painted in the colors of the four Hogwarts houses to decorate the inside.

Harry and Ron miss the train in *Harry Potter and the Chamber of Secrets*, so they fly to school in Arthur Weasley's magical Ford Anglia car. Fourteen cars portrayed the Anglia, including several used to land in the 85-foot Whomping Willow. "The Whomping Willow scene was like a theme park ride," says Rupert Grint, "and I got to drive a car!"

After their first year, students ride to Hogwarts in large carriages pulled by creatures called Thestrals, visible only to those who have witnessed death. Audiences saw the carriages in *Harry Potter and the Order of the Phoenix*, Harry's fifth year. Visual development artist Rob Bliss created three studies of the carriages, which the Thestrals pull with their tails.

In *Harry Potter and the Deathly Hallows – Part 2*, Harry, Ron, and Hermione gain access to the castle through a secret entrance behind a portrait in the basement of the Hog's Head, which is owned and operated by Professor Dumbledore's brother, Aberforth. The portrait is of Ariana Dumbledore, Albus and Aberforth's younger sister.

The Sorting Ceremony

Gryffindor!

Hogwarts castle is perched on a cliff surrounded by a forest where centaurs and giant spiders live. Within the castle, staircases move and paintings talk. But before the first feast of the school year starts in the Great Hall, first-year students must be sorted into one of four houses: Gryffindor, Slytherin, Hufflepuff, or Ravenclaw.

SC. 73
SORTING HAT.

SC. 73
SORTING HAT
(TEACHER'S P.O.V)

THE SORTING HAT

During the Sorting Ceremony, the Sorting Hat announces each first-year student's house after it's placed on their head by Professor McGonagall, who oversees the ceremony. The hat was constructed in both physical and digital forms. Dame Maggie Smith, who plays Professor McGonagall, held a leather version. To create the illusion that the hat could move and talk, each student wore just a leather brim and the top of the hat was added digitally.

FIRST YEAR GIRLS

FIRST YEAR BOYS

✳ ✳ ✳ School Uniforms ✳ ✳ ✳

The Hogwarts Acceptance Letter lists the clothing students need to bring to school, including a set of robes and a pointed hat. "[Author] J.K. Rowling said that the kids did not wear uniforms," says *Sorcerer's Stone* costume designer Judianna Makovsky. But Judianna wanted a unified look and was grateful that the filmmakers agreed with her. "Imagine trying to dress four hundred children in individual outfits!"

For *Harry Potter and the Prisoner of Azkaban*, new costume designer Jany Temime added hoods to the robes. "I wanted to link to the twenty-first century, as all kids have a hoodie," says Jany. She also created interchangeable versions of sweaters, slacks, and shirts, because "Kids want to wear things their own way."

In the later films, students wore more contemporary clothing. For this, Jany wanted to "dress them in a cool, modern way," she says, "but still have something magical about it." The majority of these "Muggle" clothes were purchased, but they were almost always altered by changing buttons, sleeves, or collars, and adding embellishments.

GRYFFINDOR

HEAD OF HOUSE:
Professor Minerva McGonagall

HOUSE FOUNDER:
Godric Gryffindor

HOUSE GHOST:
Sir Nicholas de Mimsy-Porpington (aka "Nearly Headless Nick")

FAMOUS ALUMNI:
Harry Potter (aka "The Chosen One"); Hermione Granger; Neville Longbottom; Fred, George, Ron, and Ginny Weasley (members, Dumbledore's Army)

HUFFLEPUFF

HEAD OF HOUSE:
Professor Pomona Sprout

HOUSE FOUNDER:
Helga Hufflepuff

HOUSE GHOST:
The Fat Friar

FAMOUS ALUMNI:
Cedric Diggory (Triwizard Tournament champion), Newt Scamander (author, *Fantastic Beasts and Where to Find Them*), Nymphadora Tonks (member, Order of the Phoenix)

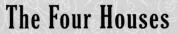

The Four Houses

Each house is named after its founder and is presided over by a current professor who can add or take points away from students in any house based on merit and behavior. At the end of the year, the house with the most points is awarded the House Cup.

Behind the Great Hall's High Table are four hourglass-shaped cylinders that contain large colored beads indicating the points won and lost by the four houses. In the films, all the beads are placed in the top compartment of the hourglasses at the beginning of each school year.

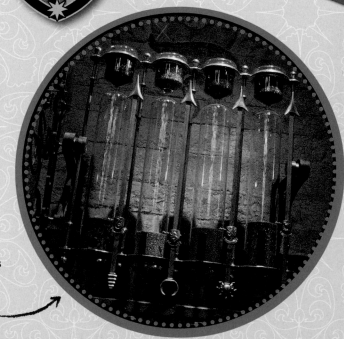

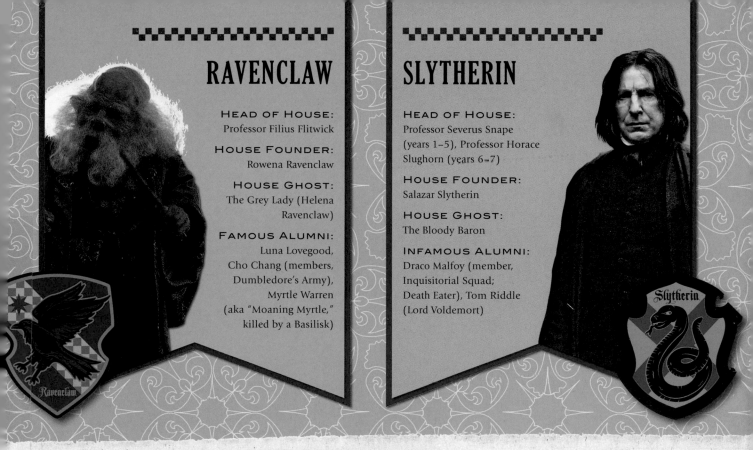

RAVENCLAW

HEAD OF HOUSE: Professor Filius Flitwick

HOUSE FOUNDER: Rowena Ravenclaw

HOUSE GHOST: The Grey Lady (Helena Ravenclaw)

FAMOUS ALUMNI: Luna Lovegood, Cho Chang (members, Dumbledore's Army), Myrtle Warren (aka "Moaning Myrtle," killed by a Basilisk)

SLYTHERIN

HEAD OF HOUSE: Professor Severus Snape (years 1–5), Professor Horace Slughorn (years 6–7)

HOUSE FOUNDER: Salazar Slytherin

HOUSE GHOST: The Bloody Baron

INFAMOUS ALUMNI: Draco Malfoy (member, Inquisitorial Squad; Death Eater), Tom Riddle (Lord Voldemort)

The Ghosts of Hogwarts

The four house ghosts appeared in costumes from different eras, all of which were made of the same material—a mesh fabric embedded with copper wire that could be shaped. "I didn't want them to look like traditional ghosts, with chiffon waving all over the place," says Judianna Makovsky.

HEADMASTER'S OFFICE

During most of the Harry Potter films, the Headmaster of Hogwarts is Professor Albus Dumbledore. Dumbledore is caring, wise, and witty, but stern when he needs to be. His affection for and faith in Harry Potter sustains the young wizard through his adventures. Dumbledore was played by Richard Harris in the first two films, and by Michael Gambon thereafter.

INTERIOR DESIGN

The set of the headmaster's office was a favorite of production designer Stuart Craig. It was designed to have three circular levels, forty-eight portraits of former headmasters on the walls, and memory cabinets that contained almost one thousand hand-labeled glass vials. Other walls were lined with hundreds of books, many of which were really rebound telephone directories. The room's fireplace had andirons topped with bronze phoenixes, which echo the room's famed inhabitant Fawkes, Dumbledore's phoenix.

TCH THIS SPACE

Stuart Craig's ideas for Dumbledore's office was
his interest in the heavens and the universe.
that made him even more impressive," says Stuart.
"So we really went for it." The headmaster's office was
filled with astronomical equipment such as astrolabes,
which observe the position of celestial bodies, and
orreries, which illustrate the movements of planetary
bodies, as well as telescopes and microscopes. "They're
beautiful objects and often made of glass, so they gleam
and glisten," Stuart explains.

Albus Percival Wulfric Brian Dumbledore

MAGICAL STUDIES

Transfiguration

CLASS REQUIREMENTS

REQUIRED YEARS: 1–5

PROFESSOR: Minerva McGonagall

TEXTBOOK: First, Second Years: *A Beginner's Guide to Transfiguration* by Emeric Switch; Third, Fourth, Fifth Years: *Intermediate Transfiguration*; Sixth Year: *A Guide to Advanced Transfiguration*.

STUDENT TO SUPPLY: A working wand

Simply described, Transfiguration is the art of turning something into something else. The subject is taught by Professor McGonagall. "I'm the one who keeps them in order," says Dame Maggie Smith, who plays McGonagall. "I care about them, obviously, but I'm really fairly fierce." The classroom scenes were shot at Durham Cathedral, which is roughly as old as Hogwarts castle.

A Class Act

Professor McGonagall is an Animagus, a person who can choose to change themselves into an animal, which is an advanced form of Transfiguration. She displays this talent in Harry Potter's first class when her Animagus form—a tabby cat—leaps off a desk and morphs into the professor. The cat, played by Mrs. P. Head, wore an invisible safety harness held by a trainer. On cue, the cat sprang up as the harness was released. This was then combined with footage of Maggie Smith to complete the transformation.

In addition to creating textbooks, the graphics department occasionally provided completed homework assignments. The one pictured above is for transfiguring worms for *Harry Potter and the Chamber of Secrets*.

Charms

CLASS REQUIREMENTS

REQUIRED YEARS: 1–5

PROFESSOR: Filius Flitwick

TEXTBOOK: *The Standard Book of Spells*, Grades 1–5, by Miranda Goshawk

STUDENT TO SUPPLY: A wand

Charms class teaches charms and spells through the combination of a wand movement and spoken incantation. Filius Flitwick, played by Warwick Davis, is the Charms professor. Warwick felt that his character was "the kind of teacher that you could go to if you hadn't done your homework, and he'd say, 'Don't worry about it. Complete it today and bring it in tomorrow.'"

SPELLS & CHARMS

SWISH AND FLICK!

In their first lesson in *Harry Potter and the Sorcerer's Stone*, students learned the "swish and flick" wand movement in order to cast the *Wingardium Leviosa* spell and levitate a feather. For *Harry Potter and the Order of the Phoenix*, director David Yates brought in "wand choreographer" Paul Harris to create the best movements to enhance a wizard's skill. "We were trying to find what made a wizard better," says Paul. "What makes a spell work better than another? If you have a better swish and flick with your wand, your spell will be better."

Defense Against the Dark Arts

CLASS REQUIREMENTS

REQUIRED YEARS: 1–5

STUDENT TO SUPPLY: A wand

In Defense Against the Dark Arts classes, students learn how to defend themselves against Dark spells, including jinxes, hexes, and curses, and they study Dark creatures, including werewolves and Boggarts. Unfortunately, Hogwarts has found it difficult to retain a DADA teacher for more than one year at a time.

A DADA homework assignment about vampire bats created by the graphics department for *Harry Potter and the Sorcerer's Stone*.

FIRST-YEAR PROFESSOR: QUIRINUS QUIRRELL

TEXTBOOK:
The Dark Forces: A Guide to Self-Protection by Quentin Trimble

Professor Quirrell, played by Ian Hart in *Harry Potter and the Sorcerer's Stone*, hides the fact that he shares his body with Harry's nemesis, Lord Voldemort. In their final confrontation, Quirrell/Voldemort soars toward Harry to get the Sorcerer's Stone, so Hart was placed in a rig that lifted and shot him forward. "It's only for a moment in the film," says Ian, "but it was the most fun."

SECOND-YEAR PROFESSOR:
GILDEROY LOCKHART

TEXTBOOKS:
The published works of Gilderoy Lockhart

In *Harry Potter and the Chamber of Secrets*, Gilderoy Lockhart, played by Kenneth Branagh, isn't shy about praising his own skills at the craft of defensive arts, though it's discovered that his greatest skill is not being entirely truthful. "Lockhart is an egotist, a show-off, and a fraud," says Daniel Radcliffe. "Girls love him, and boys hate him because they know that something is not quite right. He's cringe-worthy."

THIRD-YEAR PROFESSOR:
REMUS LUPIN

TEXTBOOK:
The Essential Defence Against the Dark Arts by Arsenius Jigger

Harry's third-year DADA professor, in *Harry Potter and the Prisoner of Azkaban*, is Remus Lupin, played by David Thewlis. "Lupin is that teacher who is a little more social and friendly than would normally be the case," says David. "He's very kindly." However, Lupin has a dark secret: he's a werewolf. "But that's something he can't control," insists David, "and when he transforms back into human form, he's back to the same old lovable Lupin."

FOURTH-YEAR PROFESSOR:
ALASTOR MOODY

TEXTBOOK:
Unavailable

Actor Brendan Gleeson found it appealing that, as a teacher, Alastor "Mad-Eye" Moody was a no-nonsense kind of guy. "He wants to show his students what they're up against. He wants them to face the fact that evil exists and they'd better face up to it. It's tough love, but in the end, of course, what you see is not what you get with Moody. He's really there to protect Harry."

FIFTH-YEAR PROFESSOR:
DOLORES UMBRIDGE

TEXTBOOK:
Dark Arts Defence: Basics for Beginners

The Ministry of Magic sends Dolores Umbridge to Hogwarts in *Harry Potter and the Order of the Phoenix* to influence the students' curriculum. "She doesn't want them to be doing any spells she thinks are dangerous," says actress Imelda Staunton, who plays Umbridge. "She feels she's absolutely succeeded in regaining control, but she's very patronizing." Emma Watson (who plays Hermione) describes Umbridge in another way: "She's a bit of a psycho, basically."

Potions

CLASS REQUIREMENTS

REQUIRED YEARS: 1–5

PROFESSOR: Severus Snape

TEXTBOOK: *Magical Drafts and Potions* by Arsenius Jigger

STUDENT TO SUPPLY: Potion ingredients, cauldron, brass scales, glass or crystal vials

In Potions class, students learn how to brew concoctions ranging from Liquid Luck to the Draught of Living Death, as well as important elixirs, tonics, and antidotes. The Potions Master for Harry's first five years is Severus Snape, a strict teacher who favors his Slytherin students.

IN CHARACTER

Severus Snape, played by Alan Rickman, is formidable and forbidding. "I'd arrive on set in full costume and makeup as Snape," said Alan. "I was very aware that the kids were confronted by the Snape-ness of me—so it took a while for them to know that there was somebody else underneath it all." Rupert Grint remembers that Alan usually stayed in character between takes. "I don't mean he was evil or anything," says Rupert, "but he was quite intimidating."

For *Harry Potter and the Chamber of Secrets*, Hermione Granger concocted the Polyjuice Potion in order to discover the identity of the heir of Slytherin. The graphics department created both a printed and a handwritten version of the potion recipe, copied from the book *Moste Potente Potions*.

Potions
(Post O.W.L.s)

CLASS REQUIREMENTS

YEAR: 6, based on O.W.L.s

PROFESSOR: Horace Slughorn

TEXTBOOK: *Advanced Potion Making* by Libatius Borage

In *Harry Potter and the Half-Blood Prince*, Albus Dumbledore brings former Potions professor Horace Slughorn back to his old position. Snape required an "Outstanding" O.W.L. to continue, but Slughorn only needed "Exceeds Expectations," so Harry Potter and Ron Weasley (reluctantly) add this class to their schedule. Dumbledore believes that a memory of Slughorn's offers a way to defeat Voldemort, and he compels Harry to get this information.

HORACE SLUGHORN

BACK TO SCHOOL

Actor Jim Broadbent characterizes Slughorn as "eccentric. He's passionate about his work. He's incredibly knowledgeable and sort of obsessive, really. Horace is a sort of teacher that we've all known who adores their pupils," Jim continues. "Teaching has been his whole life. So when he's asked to come back out of retirement, to come back to Hogwarts, he 'reluctantly leaps' at the idea, as I would put it."

PROPERTY OF THE HALF-BLOOD PRINCE

Harry discovers that his used copy of *Advanced Potion Making* belonged to Severus Snape, who wrote in the book, correcting instructions and adding his own spells and potions. Miraphora Mina did the actual handwriting. "I had to imagine how Snape would write," she says. Her thought was that he wouldn't have been neat and tidy. "He probably had it going in different directions, with lots of thinking and scrubbing out."

This book is the property of the Half-Blood Prince

Herbology

CLASS REQUIREMENTS

REQUIRED YEARS: 1–5

PROFESSOR: Pomona Sprout

TEXTBOOKS: First and Second Years:
1000 Magical Herbs & Fungi by Phyllida Spore

STUDENT TO SUPPLY: Dragon-hide gloves

Herbology is the study of magical plants. Many of these plants have medicinal benefits, so not only do the students add to their own knowledge, but their work also helps fellow classmates and teachers who become injured. In *Harry Potter and the Chamber of Secrets*, second years create an antidote from Mandrake roots that cures other students who become Petrified by the Basilisk.

Herbology is taught by Pomona Sprout, played by Miriam Margoyles. "I remember going up for the interview for Professor Sprout and being absolutely over the moon that I'd gotten the job," Miriam says. Sprout was first seen in *Harry Potter and the Chamber of Secrets*. "I was quite a dictatorial and bossy sort of character in that one," she admits. For her final appearance in *Harry Potter and the Deathly Hallows – Part 2*, "I grew rather mellower," says Miriam.

Herbology Lesson

1. How many leaves does the CIBRATE plant have?
   ❀ ❀ ○ ○ ○
   Between 20-30 depending on the age of it.

2. How many spikes does the SPIKTO CIKUS have? (fully grown)
   ✻ ✻ ✻
   100, and they are dangerous!!

3. At three months how tall is the LUNGPUSH PLANT?
   ☀ 3 ft. 1 inch, if the weather is good! ☀

4. Does the AKIMMBLE fungi go red?

A sample of Herbology homework created by the graphics department for *Harry Potter and the Chamber of Secrets*.

A FRIEND IN GILLYWEED

In *Harry Potter and the Goblet of Fire*, the second task of the Triwizard Tournament required the champions to swim under the Black Lake for a considerable amount of time. Plant enthusiast Neville Longbottom suggested Harry use Gillyweed to help him breathe underwater, as he read about it in an herbology guide.

Divination
(Third years and up)

CLASS REQUIREMENTS

YEARS: 3 and up

PROFESSOR: Sybill Trelawney

TEXTBOOK: *Unfogging the Future* by Cassandra Vablatsky

STUDENT TO SUPPLY: An open mind

First seen in *Harry Potter and the Prisoner of Azkaban*, Divination is the art of foretelling the future. Students learn methods to foresee upcoming events, including crystal ball–gazing and tessomancy, which predicts the future through the reading of tea leaves.

FUTURE SHLOCK

Professor Sybill Trelawney is played by actress Emma Thompson. "I think she's bogus, really," says Emma. "She has a genuine gift, but she has to make it stretch. She has to make it bigger than it actually is." Emma felt that though there was something faintly helpless about her character, "underneath that helplessness is steel. But then she does see really, truly frightening things."

PLACE YOUR ORDER

When set decorator Stephenie McMillan was looking for items to use in the Divination classroom, she contacted the prop department, which had catalogued and carefully stored every chair, banner, plate, and Remembrall used in the Harry Potter films. "They have storage down to a tee," Stephenie explained, "and I like the idea of recycling and reusing things." So she asked if they could locate thirty-six teapots used in the first film. "And they showed up in twenty minutes!"

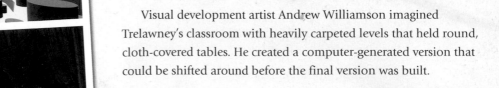

Visual development artist Andrew Williamson imagined Trelawney's classroom with heavily carpeted levels that held round, cloth-covered tables. He created a computer-generated version that could be shifted around before the final version was built.

Care of Magical Creatures
(Third years and up)

CLASS REQUIREMENTS

YEARS: 3 and up

PROFESSOR: Rubeus Hagrid

TEXTBOOK: *The Monster Book of Monsters*

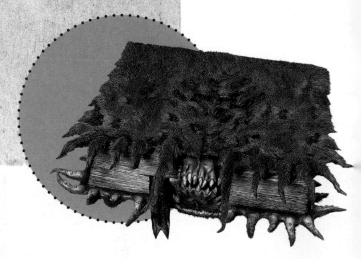

Rubeus Hagrid, played by Robbie Coltrane, becomes the Care of Magical Creatures professor in *Harry Potter and the Prisoner of Azkaban*. Hagrid is beloved by the students, but his teaching methods are sometimes questionable. "He's very kind to children, who like him because he's big and strong and kind, and that's what children want," says Robbie. "He's also very kind to animals, including some [that] other people wouldn't go within five hundred yards of!"

LESSON ONE: HIPPOGRIFFS

"Hagrid finds it exciting to be the Creatures professor," says Robbie Coltrane. "And he's got this marvelous creature, the Hippogriff," which Hagrid brings to his first class. Buckbeak the Hippogriff is half horse, half eagle. He is a very proud and cautious creature. The opening lesson combined computer technology with a full-size, radio-controlled version of the animal. When Robbie brought his five-year-old daughter to the set, Buckbeak's "handlers" had the Hippogriff rub its head on her arms. "She thought it was a new creature," he says. "She thought it was real."

Student Resources

To help with classwork and exams, and even to help students find their way to the next class, various items were offered over the course of the films by the prop and graphics departments. Some were plot-driven, while others added details to the storytelling.

For *Harry Potter and the Half-Blood Prince*, a map was created by the graphics department to help first-year students find their way around the Hogwarts grounds.

Notices are posted in the house common rooms for lost items, tutorial options, and Quidditch schedules. These notices, posted in Gryffindor's common room, were made for *Harry Potter and the Sorcerer's Stone*. The announcements changed every year.

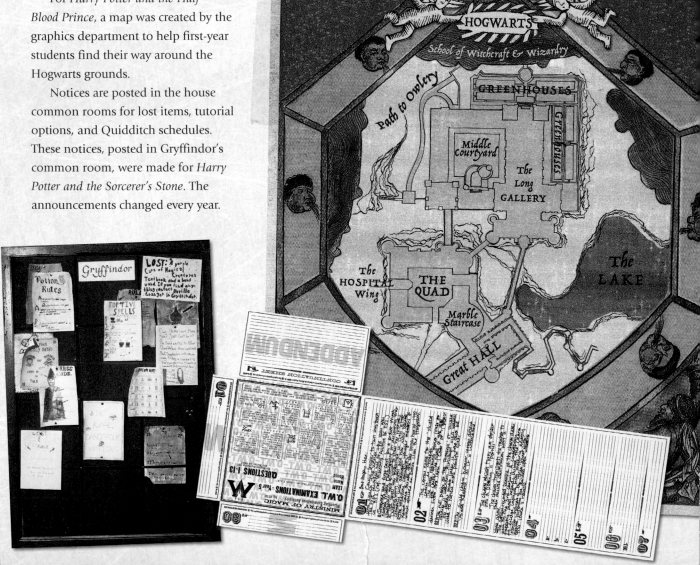

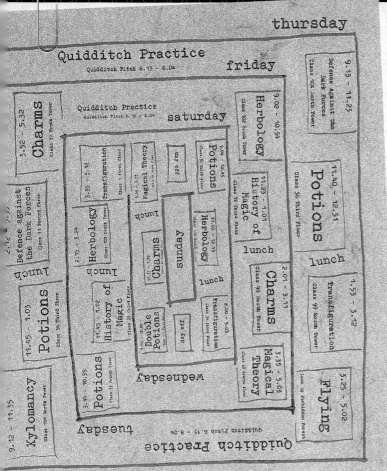

Hermione Granger takes on an overcrowded class schedule in *Harry Potter and the Prisoner of Azkaban*, seen here in a physical form created by the graphics department. The mazelike timetable even includes time to watch her fellow Gryffindors in Quidditch practice.

Hermione was given a Time-Turner by Professor McGonagall, allowing her to take two classes at the same time. The prop was created by Miraphora Mina, who was inspired by a collapsible astrolabe in Dumbledore's office. "I also wanted a moving element," says Miraphora. "When it 'comes alive,' it becomes three-dimensional, because it's a ring within a ring with a part that spins."

✦ ✦ ✦ ✥ ✦ ✦ ✦

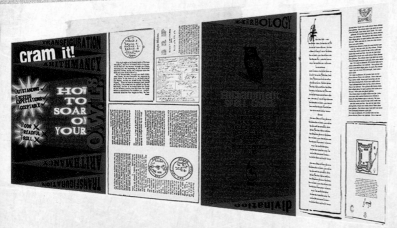

Fifth-year students can get help with a "spell check" before taking their O.W.L. exams by using *Cram It! How to Soar on Your O.W.L.s*. This one was used by Ron Weasley in *Harry Potter and the Order of the Phoenix*.

Quidditch

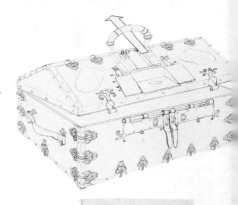

Hogwarts has an exceptional Quidditch intramural sports program. Every year, the four houses compete to win the Hogwarts Quidditch Cup. When Harry Potter joined the Gryffindor team as Seeker in his first year, he was the youngest house player in one hundred years.

The director of *Harry Potter and the Sorcerer's Stone*, Chris Columbus, knew that the game would lean heavily on CGI. "We shot the individual Quidditch players on a green-screen stage and incorporated their shots with the backgrounds. Riding the brooms was a tremendously difficult thing to do," he adds. "They had to create a sense of movement and a sense of urgency, and at the same time make it feel as if these were real athletes playing a game."

"I was looking forward to it," remembers Daniel Radcliffe (who played Harry Potter), "and then very quickly realized how much I didn't like it in those very early days when we were still working it out. It was really hard and really painful being up there for hours at a time." Fortunately, extra padding was added to the Quidditch uniforms in key places as the films progressed.

Active Wear

In the first two films, the Quidditch outfits resembled cricket garb. For *Harry Potter and the Prisoner of Azkaban*, goggles were added to protect against bad weather, the uniform material was changed to a water-resistant nylon, and numbers were added on the players' backs. "So kids could follow their favorite player," says costume designer Jany Temime. In *Harry Potter and the Half-Blood Prince*, the players wore hooded warm-up outfits in practice, and a collection of branded "fan wear" was created for each team's supporters.

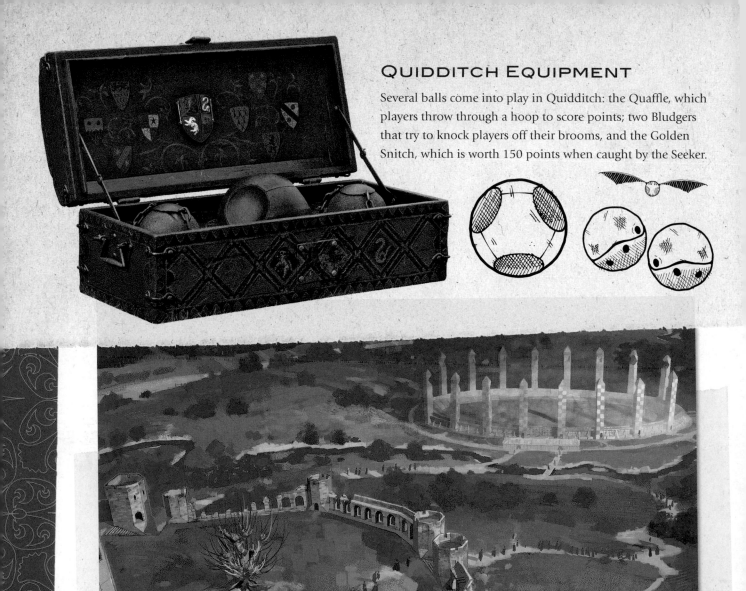

Quidditch Equipment

Several balls come into play in Quidditch: the Quaffle, which players throw through a hoop to score points; two Bludgers that try to knock players off their brooms, and the Golden Snitch, which is worth 150 points when caught by the Seeker.

"With the Quaffle, we built what we call a patent," says head prop modeler Pierre Bohanna, who used this to make molds of the game's biggest ball. Once each ball was cast in a dense foam, "We gave it a red-colored leatherette texture and stitching like an old-school heavy football. That was the general feel of all the Quidditch equipment: well used. Everything was pretty worn and knackered."

To get the right surface for the metallic Bludgers, the balls were coated with an iron powder, and then an acid was applied to give them a rusty finish. "We were quite mad going that far," says Pierre, "but it really shows in its quality."

Gold-plated physical Snitches were cast that included details difficult to see. "The Snitch has fluttering silver wings, which must be completely hidden while at rest," says production designer Stuart Craig. Pierre Bohanna's prop-making team brought concept artist Gert Stevens's illustrations to life. The Snitch has two deep, narrow channels curving across its surface. "They look like surface decoration, but they're secretly hiding the wings," says Stuart.

Official School Activities

Hogwarts offers both student- and teacher-run organizations to improve skills or share common interests.

A Dueling Club was started by Professor Gilderoy Lockhart in *Harry Potter and the Chamber of Secrets* to allow students to practice defensive wand moves. The scene was set in the Great Hall, where a covered catwalk provided the playing field. This was a favorite scene of Tom Felton, who played Draco Malfoy. "I thought it was a brilliant scene," says Tom. "That was a lot of fun, doing our own stunts at thirteen or fourteen [years old]. That was pretty exciting."

"I THOUGHT IT WAS A BRILLIANT SCENE [. . .] THAT WAS A LOT OF FUN, DOING OUR OWN STUNTS AT THIRTEEN OR FOURTEEN [YEARS OLD]. THAT WAS PRETTY EXCITING."

—Tom Felton (Draco Malfoy)

In *Harry Potter and the Prisoner of Azkaban*, we're introduced to the Frog Choir, whose members hold radio-controlled animatronic toads that croak out their song's bass line. The choir's director was played by Warwick Davis, who calls him "Professor of Magical Music." The role came about when Warwick's character of Professor Filius Flitwick didn't make it into the third film, and producer David Heyman asked if he'd like to conduct the choir performance.

The Slug Club consists of students selected by Professor Horace Slughorn based on merit in Potions class as well as family or business connections. "He sort of collects the star pupils around him," says actor Jim Broadbent, who portrays Slughorn. During the Christmas season in *Harry Potter and the Half-Blood Prince*, Slughorn hosts a club party. Luna Lovegood (played by Evanna Lynch) wore an extremely festive dress, silver slippers, and silver jewelry. Evanna made her own beaded charm bracelet, which includes her hare Patronus, for the scene.

In order to thwart a suspected student conspiracy, Dolores Umbridge forms the Inquisitorial Squad in *Harry Potter and the Order of the Phoenix*. "She has a little posse she can gather up to help her," says Imelda Staunton. "I think, in her mind, there are kids who will see her way as being 'right' before others do. And these helpers, of course, are delighted to be part of this."

✳ ✳ ✳ ✳ Unofficial School Activities ✳ ✳ ✳ ✳

DUMBLEDORE'S ARMY

In *Harry Potter and the Order of the Phoenix*, Hermione Granger realizes that Defense Against the Dark Arts professor Dolores Umbridge is not going to give her students any useful instruction. She decides that Harry Potter, who has already killed a Basilisk and produced a Patronus, should teach them what he knows.

The students try to find a place to practice away from Umbridge's prying eyes. Luckily, Neville Longbottom discovers the Room of Requirement, which can only be found by those in need of it. When the DADA students—later dubbed Dumbledore's Army—use it for practice, the Room is empty and its walls are covered in mirrors. "I felt it appropriate that it reflected you and your need back to yourself," says production designer Stuart Craig. "We did acknowledge the fact that anything they needed would be instantly provided. So when they need a 'Death Eater' to practice with, one appears." This may also explain the mistletoe that appears above Harry and Cho Chang's heads before they share a kiss.

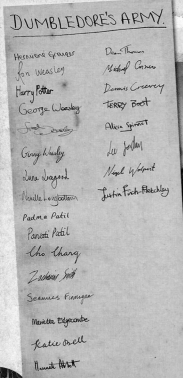

DUMBLEDORE'S ARMY.

Hermione Granger
Ron Weasley
Harry Potter
George Weasley
Fred Weasley
Ginny Weasley
Luna Lovegood
Neville Longbottom
Padma Patil
Parvati Patil
Cho Chang
Zacharias Smith
Seamus Finnigan
Marietta Edgecombe
Katie Bell
Hannah Abbott
Susan Bones

Dean Thomas
Michael Corner
Dennis Creevey
TERRY Boot
Alicia Spinnet
Lee Jordan
Nigel Wolpert
Justin Finch-Fletchley

The Room also "provided what was needed" in other films. In *Harry Potter and the Half-Blood Prince*, Ginny hid Harry's Half-Blood Prince's Potions book in the Room, which was then filled with artifacts. In *Harry Potter and the Deathly Hallows – Part 2*, the Room held hammocks for rebellious students hiding within the school and was later filled to the top with artifacts when Harry sought Rowena Ravenclaw's diadem Horcrux. "The fact that they were looking for this tiny little jewel of an object in something so massive and complicated just made the task all the more impossible," Stuart Craig explains.

Written by Jody Revenson

First U.S. edition 2018

ISBN 978-1-9848-3045-6

Published in the United States by Random House Children's Books, a division of Penguin Random House LLC, 1745 Broadway, New York, NY 10019, and in Canada by Penguin Random House Canada Limited, Toronto. Random House and the colophon are registered trademarks of Penguin Random House LLC.

rhcbooks.com

MANUFACTURED IN CHINA

10 9 8 7 6 5 4 3 2 1

IN MEMORIAM

Sadly, some members of the wizarding world have passed away since the finish of Harry Potter's screen story. These include actor Richard Harris, whose Dumbledore made us all feel loved and safe; Stephenie McMillan, set decorator for all eight films; and actor Alan Rickman, who brought the always intriguing Severus Snape to the screen. We raise our wands in tribute to these talented people who brought their magic to the Harry Potter films.

Produced by

PO Box 3088
San Rafael, CA 94912
www.insighteditions.com

Publisher: Raoul Goff
Associate Publisher: Vanessa Lopez
Creative Director: Chrissy Kwasnik
Designer: Evelyn Furuta
Editor: Gregory Solano
Editorial Assistant: Hilary VandenBroek
Senior Production Editor: Rachel Anderson
Production Director: Lina s Palma
Production Manager: Jacob Frink

Insight Editions, in association with Roots of Peace, will plant two trees for each tree used in the manufacturing of this book. Roots of Peace is an internationally renowned humanitarian organization dedicated to eradicating land mines worldwide and converting war-torn lands into productive farms and wildlife habitats. Roots of Peace will plant two million fruit and nut trees in Afghanistan and provide farmers there with the skills and support necessary for sustainable land use.